Cock-a-doodle-Moo

The story of Cock-a-doodle-moo
and all the pictures in this book are
original and have been specially
commissioned for Tesco.

Published by
Tesco Stores Limited
Created by Brilliant Books Ltd
84-86 Regent Street
London W1B 5RR
www.brilliantbooks.co.uk

First published 2001

Text © 2001 Brilliant Books Ltd
Illustrations © 2001 Charlotte Combe
Printed by Printer Trento S.r.l., Italy
Reproduction by Graphic Ideas Studios, England

ISBN 1-84221-123-4

1 3 5 7 9 10 8 6 4 2

Fun
to
LEARN

Cock-a-doodle-moo

Written by Alison Henley

Illustrated by Charlotte Combe

Farmer Bill returned home from the market one day and in his hands he carried a rooster. 'Look my dear,' he said to his wife, 'I've bought a rooster to wake us up in the morning!'

After a hearty dinner and lots of lovely pudding,
Farmer Bill and his wife settled their new rooster
in the hay barn and went to bed for the night.

'Now that we have the new rooster to wake us,
we won't need our alarm clock,' said Farmer Bill,
as he snuggled down under the duvet.

But...the next morning, the farm lay silent – the pigs didn't oink, the ducks didn't quack and the cows didn't moo. And because the rooster didn't crow... everyone overslept!

Farmer Bill had never slept in so late. His wife shook him and told him it was six o'clock. 'Six o'clock!' he bellowed. 'It can't be!' And he threw back the duvet saying, 'I must milk the chickens and shear the pigs at once!' Farmer Bill's wife knew what he meant.

'I'll cook your breakfast for
you, dear,' she called to him.
'No time for breakfast, I must
get going,' Farmer Bill replied,
racing down the stairs.

Rooster had just woken up and after having a good
stretch he wandered out of the barn to have a look
round his new home. The sun was shining brightly
and the soft breeze in the air felt good.

Rooster stood still for a while and took in
the view. 'Wow, this farm is humungous!'
Full of curiosity, he walked along the
path to see where it would lead.

He came across the sheep in their pen.
The sheep glared at him. 'Why didn't you
wake us this morning?' they bleated.
'Now Farmer Bill is running late.'

'Oh!' said Rooster. 'It's my first day.
Must I come and wake you all up?'
'No, no, that would take all day. You just
make a loud noise for all of us to hear.'
'Oh!' said Rooster. 'What sort of noise?'

poodle-baa...

'I think it goes cock-a-doodle-baa,' replied one of the sheep, nodding to herself. So Rooster went on his way saying, 'Cock-a-doodle-baa, cock-a-doodle-baa, cock-a-doodle-baa,' to himself, so as not to forget.

Baa...

Just then he spotted some pigs.
'Farmer Bill was late this morning
because of you,' grunted one of the pigs.
'Yes, I know,' replied Rooster, sadly,
'but it's only my first day. I'll wake you
tomorrow with my cock-a-doodle-baa.'

'Cock-a-doodle-baa?!
It's not cock-a-doodle-baa. It's
cock-a-doodle-oink,' insisted the pig.
'Cock-a-doodle-oink?' asked Rooster.
'Are you sure?'

'Absolutely positive,' said the pig,
rolling in the nice cool mud.

By this time, the cows were
moving out of their shed.
'Good morning,' said Rooster.
'Not much of it left thanks
to you,' complained the cows.

'Yes, I know, I must wake you all bright
and early with my cock-a-doodle...'
'Moo,' interrupted the cow.
'Well, yes, as you say,' replied
Rooster, getting very confused.
'Cock-a-doodle-moo.'

mooo.....

Rooster was so confused he couldn't talk.

He kept repeating to himself, 'Cock-a-doodle-baa.

Cock-a-doodle-oink. Cock-a-doodle-moo.'

But none of them felt quite right.

Later that day, Farmer Bill's wife baked some seed
cakes. She put them on a plate and took them to
the barn for Rooster. As she placed the seed cakes
in front of him she stroked Rooster's neck gently,
saying, 'I do hope you'll wake us in the morning.'

'So do I,' thought Rooster, but he didn't feel at all happy. What with all the cock-a-doodle-baas, oinks, and moos going round his mind, he had quite a bad headache.

But he settled himself down for the night, and with a final worried cluck, he fell into a fitful sleep.

In the morning, before anyone else
had woken, Rooster opened his eyes.
'Oh dear,' he said anxiously to himself,
'Whatever am I to do...? Do...??
Dooooo!!'

He sprang to his feet.
'That's it!' he said. 'I've got it!
It's **not** cock-a-doodle-baa
or cock-a-doodle-oink
or cock-a-doodle-moo. It's...'
and before Rooster could
stop himself he yelled...